D1105927

Journey from Guwahati to Machhiwara

Journey from Guwahati to Machhiwara

Rajiv Bakshi

Notion Press

5 Muthu Kalathy Street, Triplicane,

Chennai - 600 005

First Published by Notion Press 2015

Copyright © Rajiv Bakshi 2015

All Rights Reserved.

ISBN: 978-93-84391-75-1

This book has been published in good faith that the work of the author is original. All efforts have been taken to make the material error-free. However, the author and the publisher disclaim the responsibility.

No part of this book may be used, reproduced in any manner whatsoever without written permission from the author, except in the case of brief quotations embodied in critical articles and reviews.

The Book is dedicated to my parents M M Bakshi & Kiran Bakshi and my wife Mrinalini. Special thanks to my son Tarun who helped me in editing the book and to my daughter in law Chhavi for the images she clicked specially for the Book.

Special thank you note for the team of Notion Press Chennai who worked whole heartedly to convert my dream project into reality.

I would like to thank Almighty for His unstinted support to me.

Foreword

My cousin, Rajiv the banker, is now Rajiv the writer!

After a successful career as a banker that took him to places across the length and breadth of the country, Rajiv has turned some of his experiences into short stories.

You, dear reader, are in for a treat! The stories are short and evocative, and you can consume them like sweet or savory snacks--sample a few or many!

In these stories are reflected the day to day lives of relatives/families/friends just like yours or mine. Every now and then you may get a jolt of recognition of the fun and frolic with friends and family, and perhaps their foibles too.

I thoroughly enjoyed the stories, and know that you will as well.

Prof. Rakesh Gupta (& former Dean)
Adelphi University Garden City, NY
February 2015

Preface

How did the idea to write Journey from Guwahati to Machhiwara took place ? The day 29 Feb 2012 I retired from my favourite Punjab & Sind Bank, I did not know what to do on subsequent days after the retirement. There was no hurry to catch the bus to Samrala, Heddon or Machhiwara. There was no job to book air tickets to Srinagar or railway tickets to Jammu or Guwahati. The only work on my first day after retirement was to SLEEP soundly.

I recollected that I had written a poem Sleep when I was eight years old in Sainik School Kapurthala and the poem got published in the school magazine. This was the first time I saw my name in print. Then there was a gap of 35 long years when I was busy in pursuing my Post Graduation in English from DAV college Jallandhar. After a stint of two years in college teaching English Grammar &

Shakespeare it was a long Journey in second class compartment from Ludhiana to Guwahati in train where I read Khuswant Singhs Train to Pakistan. During the free time in Bank the spark to write short stories took place. I vouch that all stories I wrote were published in my Banks PSB House Journal.

After retirement I was encouraged to write my memoirs by my wife Mrinalini who is also Post Graduate in Literature but in a different stream. My son Tarun & daughter in law Chhavi who work in California in USA encouraged me to write more stories. They helped me editing all the stories and each story must have been edited innumerable times to make the stories readable for the readers. As such started my Second innings as an author of Journey from Guwahati to Machhiwara. Happy Reading to my unknown friends, colleagues from Bank & my relatives.

Contents

Sleep

Oh My dear please come, I want to sleep
I have worked a lot today, now I want to sleep
The time you come is very less, I want an
ample of time
Please accept my humble request, I promise I
will never forget you!!

THE BOSS is "ALWAYS" RIGHT!
Z Z Z Z Z
20 DEC '09

My First Day in Gauhati - Start of the First Innings

Never in my life I thought that my first job will be in a Bank dominated by community of Sikh people – *the most friendly people I have ever met* and that too about 2200 Km from my home town: Jallandhar. Those were the days when the trains were not super fast and it used to take around 60 hours to reach Guwahati from Jallandhar. At that time Guwahati was spelled as Gauhati. I clearly remember the date I reached Gauhati - December 24 1976 – start of my first innings in professional life. As a young ambitious boy of 24, leaving his parents, brothers, sisters, uncles, aunts and all others who come in a joint family and then travel in a second class compartment is now hard to imagine – both travelling in second class and living in joint family.

I had never been to Punjab & Sind Bank before I joined this Bank as an Officer Trainee in Fancy Bazar Gauhati. After taking a rickshaw from the railway station I was heading to a new job - my first and that too in a new environment, new people, new place and no friends and no acquaintance. I am talking about 1976 when no one had heard about facebook and whatsapp so I could not tell my loved ones of my whereabouts every minute and no snap chat to share the pictures of my exciting train journey. After working 35 years in this Bank and having traveled abroad to ten countries I have very few *real* good friends but a whole lot of facebook friends.

I reached my bank gate where I was greeted by the bank's guard – an ex Serviceman. But I did not dare to ask his name for the first fortnight. Such was his personality – His army looks and well built body with a gun in his hand at all times, approaching him to make a friendly conversation seemed to be a daunting task. Then I was told by Kuldeep Singh

Grewal, a young Officer from Narangwal that the guard's name was Shamsher Singh - a name which suited his personality.

The day came when I mustered the courage to speak with Shamsher Singh - I had practiced the *likely conversation* in front of the mirror at least a dozen times. Ofcourse it did not go as I had envisioned. The only thing which went as per my rehersal was to say hello and mentioned him my name. And after that was a bombardment of questions, one after the other, like an army general has ordered his battalion to start the continuous rounds of fires. *From where I had come? How many family members? What is my father's occupation? My Qualification? What prompted me to join this Bank and not some other Bank? Did I always wanted to be a banker? Since I had studied in Sainik school, why did I not join army?* But I must say the interview was tough and much more interesting than my previous interview in Sunder Nagar, New Delhi – my interview for the job.

From the gate I was escorted by one peon to the second most powerful man in the

Branch. He was Dev Singh, Sikh gentleman from Ludhiana. He was the Second Man of the Branch. Dev Singh was surrounded by a large battery of employees named Gurbachan Singh, Baldev Singh, Jagdev Singh Saini, Devinder Singh Gulati, Gurmit Singh Taneja & Gurmit Singh Bhutani. Later in the week I came to know that the Second Man had the power to grant Casual leave, Earned leave, light seat of the bank and sometimes a bit of furlough. Only he had to be kept *Happy*. Since it was my first job I had to call every one as Sir and had to be most courteous. I opened my bag and distributed all the sweets I had brought from Lovely Sweets Jallandhar. The entire staff, including me relished the desi ghee sweets and for a moment we all thought we were in Punjab in a sweet shop enjoying the rich sweets instead of being in one of the Seven Sisters States - Assam. One of them made a comment that enjoy the sweets for the celebration that another *murga* has joined the Bank.

It was then my turn to get introduced to the Branch Manager - Kanwaljit Singh Kathuria. I was told to first gently knock at the Cabin of Branch Manager and be ready for yet another interview – tougher than the one I had in morning with Shamsher singh. The staff was terribly afraid of him. If Mr Kathuria called any one in his cabin, the blood pressure of that employee would go up. He had a typical habit of adjusting his spectacles whenever he wanted to emphasize a point. Some of the staff members had kept a list of excuses to be told to Mr Kathuria when ever he called the staff in his cabin. The list of excuses was neatly typed by the Steno and was in everybody's pocket.

K S Kathuria my first Branch Manager heard me patiently and I told him about my family background and my Qualification and extra circular activities. Since my father was also in a different Bank he developed a soft corner for me from the very outset. On the very first day I was given the duty to prepare Drafts. The drafts were to be prepared manually. I prepared about 70 Drafts and whenever I got the Drafts prepared of Ludhiana or Jallandhar I got emotional. Only the person who has worked in such a far place will know the reason for this. In many of the Drafts the payee was wrongly written and in some cases the amount in words and figures were written wrong by the customers which had to be corrected as well.

During the lunch break I got friendly with Jaspal Singh Pinky and went to a nearby Dhaba to have lunch. The food in Paltan Bazar Gauhati was not of Punjabi taste. There was salt even in chappatis. This was the time to remember the comforts of home and I become even more homesick.

I was free from the Bank at 8 pm. It looked as if I was out of the JAIL. There was no place for me to stay. With a meager stipend of Rupees 500 per month I could not afford a decent hotel. Most of our Bank employees stayed in a Gurdwara in Fancy Bazar opposite the Bank. I was taken to the Gurdwara by Jagdev Singh Saini and was huddled in a room shared by five or six Sikh gentlemen.

The next day was Christmas and it was a Bank Holiday. But the poor staff had to be present in the Bank. My colleagues from Punjab were getting ready and I had to help them when they were getting their turbans tied. In the local Punjabi dialect it is called *Puni*. That was the toughest part then. But now after attending so many trainings, I have become skilled in doing the *Puni*.

The same day my Big Boss Kathuria had to go to Delhi for official work. He told me to come with him to the Airport in his car to see him off. I was so happy to go out of the Bank and see the Brahmputra Valley. All the HOME SICK staff of the Bank used to loiter in the streets of Gauhati and they used to go to the Railway Station especially on Saturdays and Sundays to kill their time. The arrival of the train from Punjab cheered us. And the departure of the train to Punjab made us melancholic. Every one wished they could take the first train back to their home town. *HOW MUCH WE LONGED TO GO BACK TO OUR HOME TOWN! BUT IT WAS NOT TO BE!*

Being the night of Christmas, Iqbal singh had invited us for tea – We Punjabi's don't need a reason for a party anyways. Some of us decided to walk to his house while Iqbal Singh had taken Gurmit Singh Bhutani on his cycle to his home to reach before us to help his wife with some preperations. On the way Iqbal Singh had bought some sweets. While sitting on the back seat Bhutani had consumed three fourth of the sweets on the way., while enjoying a cycle ride with his friend. When Iqbal Singh wife served the Barfi there were just four small pieces left. What an embarrassment it was for Iqbals wife. But we didn't mind and neither did Iqbal singh as he knew who was the culprit and who will be made the scapegoat to foot the money for tickets for watching the night show of Romeo & Juliet.

One can never forget ones first job and ones First Boss. It is not like the present age when the Software Engineer changes job from Infosys to Apple to IBM in a span of ten years. The older generation like us did not have the risk taking capacity to leave one job and go for the other job. After Retirement one really misses the hectic life one has had while traveling in buses, trains, auto rickshaw, taxis and planes. I had great respect for my first

Branch Manager Mr Kanwaljit Singh Kathuria of Gauhati. Now the staff of my last Branch Machhiwara District Ludhiana can only tell what they think of me as a Branch Manager ? Thus ends my JOURNEY in the Bank from Guwahati to Machhiwara. With the publication of this book, starts my second innings as a writer !

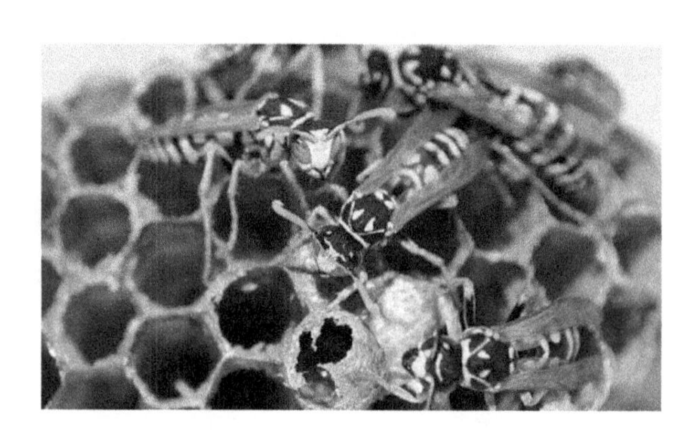

Encounter with Wasps

Once bitten twice shy. I had been bitten by wasps not once but three or four times for the past four years. While commuting even with the helmet firmly placed on my head, the wasps have bitten some times on the cheek and sometimes on the chin. The village doctor had treated me free of cost and had given 3-4 tablets to be repeated three or four times for a day or two. But this time the story was different.

After being transferred from a village branch of bank I joined a branch in an industrial area of a city. I thought my ordeal with wasps was over. I was happy that now whether I wear a helmet or not, the wasps would not trouble me. But that was not to be.

I was nominated for training for 12 days at Chandigarh in a prestigious institute. In fact I was nominated in place of another person who could not be spared due to exigencies of work. I was happy that it will be a good change for me after working so hard in a village branch.. The training started in a hi-fi manner. The main aim of the training was Motivation and how to develop leadership qualities. The training started at 7.00 am in the morning with yoga classes and ended at 8.30 pm.

Two days passed very quickly and everyone was beginning to get motivated. On the third day the pre lunch session was that of an industrialist who was telling his story from rags to riches. All the participants were thinking of emulating him.

And then it was 1.30 pm. The lunch was ready. The Director of the institute – a jolly good old man of 60 along with his industrialist friend and 25 participants proceeded towards the lawn where lunch was to be served. The van of "Mehfil" was standing outside the institute. Soup was ready to be served. The menu of the day was nicely written. God knows what, but what I remember is only “ROMALI ROTI”. The top entrepreneur of Chandigarh did not take soup but started with the food alongwith “Romali Roti”. The preparation of “Romali Roti” is a treat to watch. The young Nepali Gorkha boy of around 20 with his head smartly covered with a red apron was flouting “Romali Roti” to a height of around 2 meters. The fire was burning under a tree. A young participant did not like the height of 2 meters for roti. He said to the Nepali Gorkha: higher.

This is what I heard. At 1.35 pm I was lying on the ground. In a matter of seconds, the wasps had attacked all the participants. It must have been more than 200 wasps who surrounded the 500 meters lawn within a twinkle of eye. I do not know how the other ran for safety. But what struck me that since the wasps had literally surrounded me the best course for me was to lie on the ground. I thought my six years stay in a Sainik School will come to my rescue and I had learnt lot of motivation from my director and other high dignitaries within 2-3 days.

The wasps were biting me on my head, on my wrist, on my cheek, on my fingers and on all my parts of the body which were uncovered. Thank God I was wearing a sweater as it was winter. Not less than 60 wasps were over my body. I tried to push them away with my hand. But the more I pushed the more stings I received.

Since I was on the ground, I thought that the best course for me was to crawl for safety till the reception room of our institute. I was surprised at the participants that they had not come to my rescue. What was the use of training which was being imparted to them? I looked for an opening and tried to jump but what I saw was a 10 feet gorge. I thought I will break my leg.

I crawled and crawled and finally mustered all my courage and ran towards the main building. Then the whole action started. The Director of the Institute took full control of the situation. He pulled out a bed sheet lying on a table and wrapped the bed sheet around me. Then he gave a good thrashing to me which resulted in killing of around 20-30 wasps.

When I got a chance to look at my hand, I was flabbergasted. They looked to be hands of a WWF champion. The hospitality incharge warden brought an Avil and I galloped it down my throat.

An ambulance was arranged within 5 minutes. Five participants agreed to accompany me to the hospital. They were themselves bitten by the wasps. On reaching the hospital the first thing the doctor did was to check my B.P. and the heart beat. Then the doctor said that intravenous injections will be given. I cried for help. Never before in life had I been given intravenous injection. My friend Bhupi-a sturdy Jat Sikh from my city abused me and told me not to cry like a babe. The nurse caught hold of me and intravenous injection was given to me. And then started the "plucking out of stings". I counted myself there were around 60 stings mostly on my head, arms, cheek, wrist and one string on my thigh. I just fail to understand how my thigh was bitten by wasps.

After that started my return journey. I became a hero overnight. All the participants,

Director, teachers, employees came to enquire about my welfare. The scene of lunch had now been shifted inside the dining room. I had a full share of meals along with "Romali Roti". After having my grub I was down for a day with severe nausea, vomiting, diarrhea and slight temperature. God knows how many times the local staff of the institute including the Director came to ask about how I was feeling.

For the next 10 days I was the most "ENCOUNTERED" person. All the participants said that the first thing they will tell to their families back home will be the experience of "ENCOUNTER WITH WASPS" by one of the participants. The institute people said that this is the first and perhaps the last time that this "ENCOUNTER" of strange type has taken place.

I for once have decided not to eat "Romali Roti" again and also not to "substitute" anyone for training.

PS : Never ever have an Encounter with unknown !!!!

I WISH I WERE YOUR SHAVETA

The idea to write this story came about twenty years back. I am real jealous of her. She came to my life not as a daughter, or friend or neighbors daughter but as my Sister-in-Law's daughter.

Ever since she was born in a small hill station Dalhousie she was the most pampered child of her parents. Which daughter or son is not the pampered child of his or her parent. *Only the poor HUSBAND is not the pampered one.*

She had studied in Sacred Heart Convent School in Dalhousie and had a secret desire to settle abroad after marriage.

The first ladder to achieve her dream came when she joined a prestigious college in Jalandhar where I was also working in a nationalized bank. She wanted to stay in the hostel in spite of the fact that she was given an open invitation by my wife to stay with her. She must be fifteen or sixteen when she landed in Jallandhar. She was one of the most home sick children I had ever seen. Whenever she came to stay with us in Model Town, she was a VIP. Since she was staying away from her parents and brothers she was looked after very well by my wife and she was loved by all. Sundays and Holidays were real treat for Shaveta and my son, Tarun, who is five years younger to her.

Shaveta was given Bread Pakoras, Burgers, Rasgoolas and so many other sweets whenever she visited us. On the other hand I was just given bread omelet and that too without cheese, without butter, and top of it minus the tomato ketchup. When her mood was off or homesick, she was pampered to the full and was given gifts, her favorite food cooked.

I am real fond of food, things which I like I can eat anytime be it early morning or midnight. So I thought of using the same technique with my better half, so that I can enjoy some of my favorite food items. I did a little drama of being low one day and prompt came the reply – *"Get yourself in high sprits soon as you have to take Shaveta for shopping"*.

This made me JEALOUS of her. I had to bribe both Tarun and Shaveta to give me some Bread Pakoras or cheese rolls. The children were so happy to receive ten rupees as their extra pocket money so that they can go to the model town market and enjoy at their favorite shop.

It was the end of her stay in Jalandhar after four years. She left her hostel, college friends and all of us with a heavy heart. A few months after coming from Dalhousie and regularly visiting our place had made her feel very comfortable with us. Shaveta completed her MBA from Simla and eventually married an Investment Banker from Mumbai. Now fifteen years after her marriage she is a happy mom of a beautiful princess and a handsome prince.

A few months back when I met Shaveta and her children at Ludhiana she told her children about the golden time she spent with me at Jalandhar so many years back.

She clearly remembered the old days when she used to burst the crackers and have so many sweets on the Diwali festival.

She is one of my favorite nieces which led to the following comment to my better half from me *I wish I were your Shaveta* so that I was pampered, get lots of gifts, things to eat and no work to do after my retirement.

The Indian Love Story

This story dates back to the years 1960's when very few Indians used to go to America for higher studies and work. Since Yoginder, also known as Yogi had done his engineering from BITS Pillani and his father was a District and Session Judge in Jallandhar, he was quite comfortably placed. Yogi was youngest of the three siblings. His mother had passed away while he was fourteen. His father Sher Singh had not remarried for the sake of his children.

With a heavy heart Yogi left for greener pastures in USA. He did his Masters in Engineering from New York and was employed as an Engineer in IBM. Those were the years when children were afraid of their parents. When one day Yogi wrote to his father in

Jalandhar that he was in love with an American girl named Doris and wanted to marry her, the father lost no temper in scolding his sibling. Yogi was a young handsome boy with blue eyes and belonged to a high family of Punjab. There was no dearth of Indian girls for him. It was the time of no internet, no twitter and no Face Book. A phone call to America took long time to mature.The only source of communication was through letters which took almost fifteen days to reach and not like the present age where with a click a mouse the mail reaches the other part of the globe. Yogi convinced his father in marrying to Doris. Yogi's father could not afford to visit his son in America for his marriage. Yogi and Doris had quietly wedded in a Church. With the love Doris had for Yogi, she decided to have her name changed as Deepa for her extended Indian family. With the change in name, Doris alias Deepa, her heart also changed. She decided to familiarize herself with the Indian C's - customs, curry and culture. She wrote long letters to her relatives in India and made her place in the hearts of her Indian relatives. Doris was blessed with a son and three daughters who were all too attached to their papa Yogi and Mom Doris.

The life passed smoothly with change of job in two or three companies and change of residence from New York to Phoenix and then Florida. Yogi, Doris were in constant touch with their Indian relatives. Yogi and Doris visited Jallandhar almost five years after their marriage. They were completely bowled over by the Indian hospitality. They traveled to places like Dalhousie, Agra, New Delhi, Jallandhar and Mumbai visiting some friends and relatives. Doris adapted to the Indian culture and learnt some Indian words like: Chai, Namasate, Sabzi. Doris stayed with her father-in- law and extended family in laws. She stayed in India for six months tasting the delicacies of Indian curry, Indian sweets, Indian traffic (it was not that crowded in those times) and Indian religion. She even attended a few Indian marriages and went to the religious temples and Gurudwaras.

Everything seemed to be going well till it was not. It was almost twenty years after their marriage that one day when Yogi went to the Doctor for his check up, he was detected with Cancer of stomach. The children Dave, Indy, Neena and Sundy were too small to understand all this. The Doctor had given some hope with dose of chemotherapy. Chemotherapy was administered to Yogi for a few months but he could not survive. Yogi's father was devastated. He could not think that his son was no more. But Doris sent air ticket to her father- in-law and Sher Singh stayed at Doris place for around three months. The Indian father-in-law American daughter-in-law duo visited various cities in USA and during his stay and their connection grew deeper. She proudly introduced him as Yogi's father.

Sher Singh returned back to Jalandhar and he passed away at the age of seventy two, while his son Yogi was snatched at a young age of forty six.

Doris was left with a small family pension. But she was a lady with strong courage, positive attitude. She looked after her children very well and got them good education. She had a large family of her five sisters to support her. Some of them even asked her to remarry. But Doris, still strongly bonded with her Indian husband, said a complete no. She was committed to her children. Deepa as she was known to her Indian relatives continued to communicate with her Indian relatives. She wrote long letters to her husband's brother family and other family members. After email and Face Book became popular, she was the first one to give beautiful comments. The picture uploaded may be good, bad, ordinary but she gave such witty comments that came straight from her heart. The children of the next generation were too much attached to her. Deepa knew about the likes and dislikes of all her nephews and nieces though she had never met any one in person. Every one got a special Birthday Blessing from her.

On her seventy fifth Birthday she had celebrated a grand reunion. Around seventy relatives of her had come to attend this function. She had made it a point to see that all: her son, daughter, son-in-law, daughter-in-law and even great grand son and great grand daughter were comfortable. Her equation was different with different people. But one thing was common- THE BOND OF FAMILY.

As Doris got older, she moved her residence from damp Eugene to sunny Florida. At Eugene her daughter Indy stayed. But due to health reason she chose Florida. Almost one year after she celebrated her seventy fifth Birthday, the Face Book was flooded with pictures of herself with different relatives.

Doris daughter had mailed her Indian cousins and American cousins to send her old pictures. She had told her cousins that she had very sad news to share. The Doctor had diagnosed that she was suffering from cancer and she had decided not to take any medicine. Since she was in hospital all her children Dave, Indy, Neena & Sundy had come to see her. Doris only wanted loving glances from her family members. Two of her sisters were also with her. The Indian relatives were devastated with this mail. They rushed old pictures to Indy and Neena. Every one wanted to be with Doris.

Next day the following poem appeared on FaceBook

"Slow down Mummy there is no need to rush,

Slow down Mummy, what is all this fuss?

Slow down Mummy make yourself a cup of tea.

Slow down Mummy, come and spend some time with me.

Slow down Mummy, let's put our boots on and go out for a walk.

Let's kick at piles of leaves and smile and laugh and talk.

Slow down Mummy, you look so ever tired

Come sit and snuggle under the duvet and rest with me a while.

Slow down Mummy, these dirty dishes can wait.

Slow down Mummy, let's have some fun, let's bake a Cake!

Slow down Mummy I know you work a lot but sometimes Mummy, it's nice when you just stop.

Sit with us a minute and listen to our day.

Spend a cherished moment.

Because our childhood is not here to stay"

After reading this highly emotional poem we know what was in store for us -

The Indian Love Story had come to an end.

PS: The emotions all over the world are the same.

The Samjhauta Express

Razia was not been born with a silver spoon in her mouth. Her father - Abbaji as she used to call her, had taken all the pains to get her educated in Delhi. She was born and brought up in Delhi with circle of good friends and like any other college person, she had enjoyed her life to the fullest. After her post graduation in English, she got married to a Muslim boy, a legal expert in a bank.

Razia had only one wish in her life and the thought of not getting it fulfiled would trouble her. There was a strong desire for Razia, who had never met her brother Imran. Imran had stayed with his paternal grandparents in Pakistan at the time of partition. Razia's father had shifted to India after going through lot of trials and tribulations associated with partition. He had seen it all. He had been a spectator of seeing the Hindus being killed by Muslims and Muslims being killed by the Hindus. Razia was 2 years old when she came to India, a year elder to Imran.

Abbaji had sworn that he will never again visit the place of his birth Multan in Pakistan. There was lurking fear in his mind that something bad will happen if he decided to visit the place again. So for the sake and well being of his family – both older and younger generation he had made a promise to himself to keep it as long as he would live.

Her father, being a strict person, she could never defy him. Many times she would bring the topic to meet his brother but it was shot down right away. Only after he passed away at the ripe age of 80 the thought of meeting her brother Imran came to her mind.

Razia had found a suitable match for her daughter, Shaheen. She now wanted to personally visit Pakistan to invite her brother Imran and his family to attend marriage at

Delhi. Razia had coaxed her husband to get her visa for ten days to Pakistan. Getting visa for Pakistan was a big issue for her. Only when the marriage card was shown to the visa granting authorities of Pakistan Embassy she got the visa. But there was a hitch. As Razia's husband could not get no objection certificate from his bank in time, he could not get the visa. Razia had decided to embark the journey all by herself in the Train to Pakistan.

Razia was very excited to meet her brother for the *first* time. Razia's college friends who always knew about this pain were equally delighted and happy for Razia. They helped her in buying presents for Razia's brother's family who stayed in one of the posh areas of Lahore. Razia's friends had given her a long list for shopping in Anarkali Bazar of Lahore.

The D Day arrived. Razia was seen off at New Delhi Railway Station by her husband, daughter Shaheen and friends. Razia had already phoned her brother Imran to receive her at Lahore railway station.. It was *first* time Razia was traveling abroad and that too all alone. The excitement of meeting Imran and his wife, nephew and nieces was visible on her face. She was given lot of instructions by her husband and relatives that how she should stay in Pakistan.

Imran had promised his sister Razia that she will feel at home at her brother's residence. Though they were going to meet for the first time but the feelings of both Razia and Imran were such that they had met hundred of times. Razia had taken lot of presents from India for her relatives whom she was going to meet for the *first* time.

At Attari check point railway station the custom authorities had taken long time to check the luggage of all the passengers. The train at Attari is to be changed and all the passengers were to embark on the new train "The Samjhauta Express" which was to take them to Lahore. The very feeling that you will be in another country just after the train journey of one hour can only be felt. Razia was getting such feelings for her brother Imran.

Imran on the other hand experienced more subtle feelings. He was there to receive

Razia –his sister whom he had never seen. He had only heard her sweet voice on telephone. The day had come when she will be there on platform no 1 of Lahore station at 8.10am.

Imran has asked his driver to come at 6 am on that day. He had to visit a mosque on that day before going to railway station. All his appointments for the next ten days were cancelled. He was only there to look after his sister Razia. Imran, his wife, his children all dressed in new clothes were there with bouquets, sweets and dry fruits to welcome their guest from India.

Time and again he was looking at his watch and asking the porters about coach no 1B. Just as the train arrived, Imran saw his sister Razia waving to him in her bright red suit. He hurriedly ran to coach 1B to embrace his sister Razia. The brother sister duo of Razia-Imran embraced each other and cried. They met for the *first* time in their life and that too on a foreign soil. Both could not control their emotions along with their other family members. At this hour Imran suffered a severe heart attack and was no more thereafter.. Razia did not even know how to react. The only desire she had in her entire life was to meet *Bhai jaan*, and when it happened, life had something else planned.

It was as if Allah had arranged their meeting for the last journey of Imran.

Me and my Mobile

It was the best of times to buy Mobile.. The Prime Minister had it. 'Prerna" of "Kasauti Zindagi Ki" flouts 3310 Noika Model. The bus driver had it. The conductor who was getting a salary of Rs. 10000 could not live without it. Heights of heights husband of our maid Roshni also had it. Four years back when it was not common to have it and was considered a status symbol. I had decided that it was a sheer waste of time and waste of money.

But now after 4 years the times have changed. It is the worst of time to buy Mobile. The "AirTel" connection has crossed 1 million marks in Punjab. With so many schemes - Freedom 150, Freedom at Midnight, Prepaid, Post Paid, the glossary is ambiguous. Get mobile for Rs. 3500/- and get recharged coupons for Rs. 3240/- proclaims one of the ad's. Hutch, Orange, Spice, AirTel, BSNL, MTNL, WLL, M2M, M2 Landline, Landline 2M, there is so much confusion about the various agencies who have spread their network in the whole of country that now it is impossible to say "NO".

I had said that I don't want Mobile. But now when I travel in bus from Ludhiana to Rara Sahib and when I miss the bus by a whisker, the next day conductor of Chahil bus says "Manager Sahib you should have called me on mobile. I would have stopped the bus". I had to cut sorry figure that I did not have Mobile. Another time when my better half was furious on the maid for not coming to our house for a few days she casually said "Mam didn't you have our mobile number. I get lot of incoming calls daily". I again had to cut a sorry figure.

A few days back I was coming in a Rickhsaw with a friend of mine. The Mobile bell was ringing playing DD LJ tune. My friend put his hand in the coat. The rickshaw waala snapped back. "Sir it is not your mobile which is ringing but I am being called by my wife from Bihar". Again a sorry figure!!!

Every second good customer to our branch has a mobile. They always ask for my phone number or mobile number. If I give them my landline phone number they give me a dirty look. I knew what they mean. A Bank Manager not having mobile. They cannot believe it.

When Govinda can ask Karishma Kapoor "What is your MOBILE NUMBER", Mihir Calling Tulsi every now and then, Om calling Parvati and Shruti on Mobile *Why could not I ?*

Never mind the average bill one has to shell on mobile but I think now it has become a STATUS (Sic) symbol. The other month I was on training to Noida. There I spotted a girl having two Mobiles in her hand. I casually mentioned it to my wife. She promptly said that one Mobile was for her parents and the second one was for her B.F.

At least I have also now decided to purchase one Mobile. The "limit" comes handy for us bankers. Whenever we need something we have our "limit" to bank upon. Now we have four Mobiles in our family. One Mobile is with my son who is in Mangalore. One Mobile is with my wife. One Mobile is with me. And the fourth Mobile is for "EMERGENCY" if there is a breakdown. You can well imagine the monthly bill on Mobile. I think it is for this purpose that the bank has granted us "LIMIT".

P.S. : Dhirubhai Ambani after his death went to Heaven. He was curious to know from Anil Ambani and Tina Ambani about his company "RELIANCE" and the Rs. 501 Scheme. When Dhirubhai talked to Anil on Reliance Cellphone, Anil said "Papa our Reliance Customers are growing by leaps and bounds. But I cannot properly hear your voice. Let me talk to you from my AirTel connection".

Can we live without Mobile these days ? Think again ! May be yes ☺

Resolutions are made to be Broken

Resolution of a five year kid:

I am not going to be late for school today

Resolution of a young executive:

I am not going to be late for office today

Resolution by a young wife on her hubby's Birthday:

I am not going to pester my husband with my demands

Resolution of a forty years old man:

I am not going to drink

One can think of hundreds of resolutions and one will find that on paper and on the day of the resolution they look very attractive and hi-fi. But only after a few days they are broken like a house of cards.

The most broken resolution is by a Politician. He vows in front of 50000 strong crowd that he has been born and brought up in Culture of Party A. But a few days after he is given a plump ministerial post in Party B, he forsakes Party A and breaks his resolution and joins the bandwagon of Ministers of Party B.

The resolution by an actor and actress are also one of the glariest examples of being broken. An actress will resolve that in future she will not act in a film with Director X, and a few days later it comes to light that the same actress is going to marry Director X.

The resolutions by husbands and wife are usually broken on the very first day they are made. A husband promises that he is not coming late from office from tomorrow.

But the next day the poor chap is so busy in office that he is slogging till 8 pm. So in order to get a bit of KICK, he goes to a restaurant and has a couple of drinks and reaches home at 11 pm. Where has his resolution gone? It has gone down the drain. He again makes a resolution on that night only but it gets broken on the very next day. Thus the vicious circle moves on.

The resolutions made by a wife are usually shattered before they are made. She resolves that she will be prudent in spending money from the next month. But the resolution gets broken the day she receives the salary from the hubby dear. She joins a kitty party on the first of the following month and has to pay Rupees 5000 per month. The poor husband has to take loan every month or he goes for a loan from Citi Bank where he has to pay interest at 24 percent per annum. Or the husband takes loan from his friends or relatives.

The wife resolves that when the husband comes home he will be treated to nice cup of tea with snacks. But when he comes to his home, he is rebuked by her that he must mind his physique, He is getting over weight and what not. The husband is not helping in household chores. He is busy in only TV and Internet.

Both the husband and wife resolve that they have had enough fights and now on their marriage anniversary which falls on March 25, they are driving out to some hill station for a change. But this resolution is also broken because in the month of March the poor husband gets only Rupees ten thousand as carry home salary and the rest of money has gone for making investment to save income tax.

A man resolves that he is not going to have drinks as it is bad for his health. But on the same day the Boss is transferred and on his relieving party the drinks are served. The poor guy can not resist the offer and the resolution gets broken.

A student of tenth class resolves that he is going to work hard for his examination and not to waste time in future. But the resolution is broken when on Cable the movie Queen is being screened. Papa, Mama, Didi are going to a multiplex to see Happy New Year. How can you expect the young brat to study?

An employee comes late to the office daily. He has a readymade excuse daily. The

Boss rebukes him. The employee resolves that he will come to office on time. The next day he gets ready for office at 9 am. The poor guy starts on bike and on the way he is signaled by one of his female acquaintance to drop her at office which is about 20 kilometers from this place. What else could he want?. The girl reaches her office in time at 10 am while the poor man reaches his office at 11 am.

There are hundreds of other resolutions which are broken almost on the very day they are made. I have classified the BROKEN RESOLUTIONS under the following five categories:

1. Resolutions broken before they are made.
2. Resolutions broken on the day when they are made ie within 12 hours.
3. Resolutions broken within 24 hours.
4. Resolutions broken within a month
5. Resolutions those are never broken.

If all people make resolutions (SIC !!!) and they fall under the fifth category then we will be in a stage of utopia and we can proudly say "Achhe Din aa rahe hain"

Can you find a person who has never broken a single resolution in his life and fits in category five?

Indian Bangles
Murano Glass Pendants
Murano Glass

Husbands - Beware Do Not Shop

Sometime around early 2000, I had the luxury of getting reprieve from Punjab heat in June to visit Srinagar on a long official tour for 10 days. After finishing the Vigilance Inspection at 4 branches, I was free on the last day of my stay in Srinagar. Getting a free day during the official visit is a very happy feeling, even though some people think that I hardly work in my job but I know it I work hard. The debate of me working hard vs hardly working will continue forever like a *Coffee Toffee – Toffee Coffee* ad way back in early 1990's. Coming back to the topic at hand, I decided to try my hand at shopping on the *free* day. Money is no problem for a banker because the bank has given us “limit” so we do not have to see whether the paycheck has been received or not. If we have a limit of say Five lac and our debit balance is Four lac we can easily shop for One lac. It is another matter that for every Five lac debit balance we have to dish out more than five thousand as interest per month. In other words our salary gets reduced by five thousand. Conversely the money, which we were to get at the time of retirement, will be less by five lacs.

Anyways since it was the first time I decided to shop for my family without thinking too much on the financial impact of my deeds. I went to a big shop in Lal Chowk and the proprietor who spoke excellent English lured me to buy suits and sarees for my better half. I had decided to buy one suit but the proprietor cum salesman cajoled me for buying at least 4-5 suits. Coming to Srinagar and not buying anything! What a shame!

Karim showed me Handmade suits, Embroidered suits, Machine embroidered ones, Chiffon suits, Chinon suits, Cotton suits, Warm suits, Kashmiri suits etc. ranging from Rs 1000 to Rs 1500. After a lot of bargaining the price was settled and KarimBhai offered me rebate of 50% on all suits since I had come from Punjab and was on holiday, as he thought. My joy knew no bounds when I calculated that each suit will give me a saving of Rs.500 to Rs.750. I thought that if I purchase ten suits at rate of Rs.500 per suit I will make a clean profit of Rs.5000 in this deal.

First time in my life I mustered courage to do so much SHOPPING. I told KarimBhai that I did not have so much cash. He told me over a cup of tea that even a cheque will do. He had come to know that I was a Banker and a Banker's cheque will hardly fail. He knew all about Section 138 of Negotiable Instruments Act and the consequences a drawer faced when the cheque is returned on account of "Insufficient Funds".

I purchased ten suits for Rs.5000/- for my wife, sister, sister in law, nieces feeling delighted and thinking that that I made a good bargain. Not satisfied with this shopping I went to a leather emporium, where I spotted beautiful purses. These were all in the range of

Rs.600 to Rs.1000. On some men purses I saw the trademark "Woodlands" written. When I asked for the price from the salesman Abdul Rashid, he said that in a proper showroom of Woodlands in the land of five rivers i.e. Punjab it will cost no less than Rs.1500. But here since they were the manufacturers of the purses I will be given 50 to 60% rebate. The purse will be mine for Rs. 500 and I again mustered some courage and did shopping worth Rs. 4000 collecting purses for myself, my son and some family friends and relatives.

Two big shopping spree in a day and I was loving it, I can now imagine when the ladies shop tirelessly and with much enthusiasm every day of the week with a big smile. Next day was my flight from Srinagar to Jammu. With so much of luggage I had to do yet another shopping - a suitcase and handbag to pack my previous day shopping items. I just checked in at airport five minutes before the boarding time of 12.45P.M.

There is so much of checking, frisking of passengers, traffic rush that it takes minimum two hours to reach the airport from the main city. When the luggage was weighed it turned out to be more than the prescribed free luggage, I had to pay extra money for extra luggage. This was turning out to be quite an affair.

When I reached home I was very happy that I did so much shopping and it will be appreciated. I opened packets after packets in the morning. There were pungent comments that the embroidery was too small or it was too big. The color of the shirt did not match with the salwar or the dupatta was of different color.

Then came the turn of opening purses. The purses were too long or too short. These were not fit to be taken to the school. Or the purses were too girlish!

Oh come on, I had spent an entire day shopping and feeling good about it and end result was my family, even though appreciating the effort was not loving the items. Of course I was disheartened and irritated and I decided once for all not to shop again. It was supposed to be one of the boldest decisions of my life. But HUSBANDS BEWARE DO NOT

SHOP. Shop only for the goods you need. I had bought one Blue "Khan" suit for myself and it was one of the best shopping I had done for myself. When my wife was away to school, I collected all the suits and purses and gave them to one of the shopkeepers who had a beautiful showroom in the city. I told him to sell these goods at any reasonable price and give me the money back. Just after a week I got a message on my mobile that all these items were selling like hot cake and I had made a profit Rs. 5000 in the bargain.

Now my wife is asking me when I am going to Srinagar again ?

But lesson learnt the hard way – *No shopping please !*

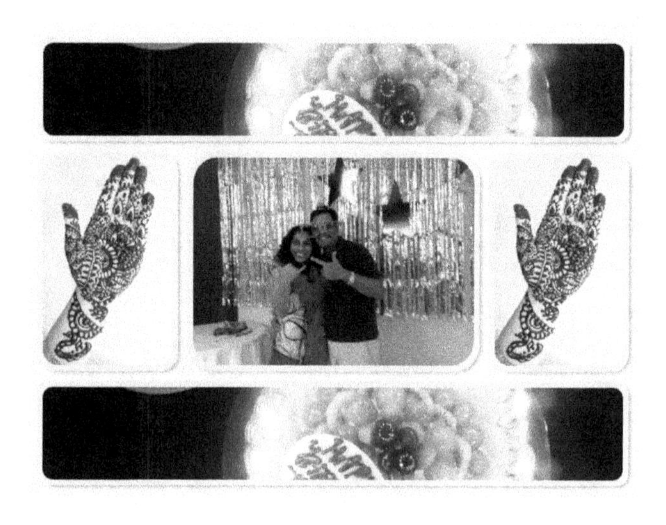

Birthdays, Marriage Anniversary & Karva Chauth

I don't know my dear readers that for how long you have been married. But I can tell you from my own experience and those of my friends, relatives and acquaintance that buying a new suit, a new sari, a new dress for even a very small occasion comes in the mind of the fairer sex very often.

In the first year of your marriage, your wife has enough clothes. She has enough suits, saris and skirts. She does not demand more dresses because the poor husband spends minimum 50 percent of his salary on paying for his accommodation and 25 percent for car or scooter loan installments and rest for food, entertainment and ration. Where is the money for buying new clothes and new dresses?

With the passage of time in marriage the demands of the wife increases from day to day. One year after his marriage, the husband out of his love and affection for his wife buys and presents her a suit for Rupees ten thousand. Even after shelling out so much money the wife does not like her dress. She is in no mood to repeat this dress at any second function. If the wife has worn a new suit for her Birthday, she will never wear the same dress on for her niece birthday. The niece at the time of attending her Massis Birthday was five years old, who wont even remember or care what her massi was wearing. As long as the cute princess gets her birthday present, she does not really care.

The poor husband has to go to various banks and LIC offices or Post Offices to get his FDR discounted, or get the lien marked on the LIC Policies or withdraw money from the Post Office after paying some discounted charges. The poor husband had saved a lot of money before his marriage. He was happy with three or four trousers and an equal number of slim fit shirts. There was no qualm of wearing the same black pant twice, three times or even four times a week.

With the passage of time the husband in order to please his wife more often increases the number of gifts in a year from one to two. The husband now makes it a point to give one suit to his wife on her Birthday and second suit on her marriage anniversary. But the quench for the suits, saris and skirts still remain.

These days most of the women are working and earning pretty good. But how many of them are contributing in the household expenditure? Usually the wife's salary goes out for buying gold, diamond set, scooter, car or the bigger car. She has to pay loan installments from her salary to a nationalized Bank.

Almost a decade after the marriage, the wife gets a new dress for her Birthday, Marriage anniversary and Karva Chauth (fast kept by the ladies for the well being of their husband). These days the husbands are considerate to pay out of their hard earned money the luxury of three suits in a year. If the suit demanded by the wife is a Designers suit, then the poor hubby has to feel the burnt. A Nalini sari above the range of Rupees ten thousand is just OK type for the considerate wife!

Three suits in a year for his wife, no husbands minds may be he is a Banker like me or any other government official. But what to do if the wife is working in a school or working as a Doctor and she has to attend a kitty party every month. She needs a special and new dress for each outing. Besides this there are so many other functions and marriages in their circle of friends which they have to attend every year. Every lady wants a new sari on a marriage of her relatives. If the marriage has three or four functions like Shagun, Cocktail, Reception then she needs a new dress for each function.

One can imagine the expenditure of the poor husband in that month.

If the wife is working in a prestigious school and she has to give a speech in front of the Chief Guest at schools annual day, a new sari is a must. Even for judging a dance competition of a KG class, new dress for that teacher is a must. The best part was when Mr Mehra told me that his wife Ritu who was working in a reputed school in Ludhiana was going for picnic to the Science City near Jallandhar and she demanded a new sari for this outing !!!

PS: Hats off to the husbands for fulfilling the small demands of their wives.

Morning Tea @8.12 am

My friend Alok had just retired from a nationalized bank as a Senior Manager in the leap year-2012. He is a gentleman in the perfect sense. His son is working as a Project Manager in IBM and also daughter- in-law, in Apple. Alok's wife is from a hill state and is working as a Principal in a prestigious school in Ludhiana. Alok has no regrets in his life. He makes it a point to give all his salary to his wife so that he is tension free. After his retirement he is giving his entire pension to his wife keeping a meager amount of Rs.500 for his monthly *'kharcha'*.

The total funds which he got from the Bank have been kept in the shape of fixed deposits for which my friend is getting substantial amount of monthly interest. What Alok needs every month is, Rs 5500 for his car expenses and Rs 1500 for his mobile bill. The rest of the money goes to the better half for her kitty.

Ever since he retired from the bank, he is trying to look for a suitable job in the private sector. One who has worked as a Senior Manager in a Nationalized bank will not go for a job in a *Laala company* even if he is offered a job of Rs 50000 per month. The Banker is used to a glass of water covered with coaster at 10am. After this, tea time at 11:30 am with his staff or customers. High Deposit customer means bread pakora or paneer pakora from Kalra sweets shop or from Pannu De Pakore shop. With Boss's visits at the Branch, then it's time for a lavish lunch from Baba chicken, so on and so forth. At 2.15 pm it is lunchtime with staff and back to work at 3 pm.

My friend Alok had a chance to open a prestigious new branch in one of the suburbs of Ludhiana. The area was flooded with money. My friend achieved the target of deposit and advances for March 2012 in the month of February 2012 after 8 months of opening the branch.

After retirement no more worry for my banker friend. No getting up early in the morning at 5.30 am to catch the 8.12 am bus from the bus stand. No worry to get the leave from office. No worry to tell Mr. Walia or Mr. Khurana that the Senior Manager will be on leave for three days to visit his friend in Gurgaon for his daughter's marriage. Retired life is a big boon for my friend Alok.

But what Alok has not been able to digest is the meager (sick!) amount of pension he gets. His friends in Army in the rank of Colonel are getting Rupees 60000/- per month. PAU Professor gets more than Rupees 50000/-per month. The poor banker is ashamed to tell his pension vis-à-vis his friends from other departments.

It was God sent opportunity when new Chief Manager Khurana joined the same bank. He was staying away from his family in New Delhi but living close to Alok in Ludhiana. Alok got close to him. Khurana once committed the greatest mistake of his life by serving handmade tea to Alok. The tea made from powdered milk reminded Alok of his days when he was posted in Guwahati, Dibrugarh and Jorhat as an Officer. Now Alok visits Khurana daily at 8.12am to have his morning quota of tea. The Pension of retired Senior Manager has increased by Rupees 250/- per month (if we take cost of tea @ Rupees 10/- per day). It is not as if my Banker friend cannot afford tea at his house. He takes tea at 6.30 am and second at 7.45am.. But the tea taken at 8.12 am is the sweetest in every sense. The tea at 6.30am is prepared by my friend's wife and at 7.45 am by his maid servant and at 8.12am by the Chief Manager (soon to be the Zonal Manager of the bank). A few days back Khurana had to go for Bank's training at Noida for 6 days and the POOR BANKER was suffering from **DEPRESSION** that this month his **PENSION** has been reduced by Sixty rupees!!

PS: Pension is the life line of Retirees.

THE GOOD SAMARITAN

Anubhav was working in Agriculture University of Ludhiana as a Stenographer. Besides working in this prestigious university he was also supplying milk on his scooter for the last thirty years to his customers. This had been his family business and he was not ashamed to do this work. Be it Sarabha Nagar in Ludhiana or Raj Guru Nagar he was ready to oblige his customers even in the biting cold in the month of December or in the sultry weather of June. At exact 7 am he was dot on time at our house with his containers of milk. He would bell the main gate and if there was no response he would quietly enter the kitchen and put milk in the utensil and neatly cover it with a plate. I had been witness to this routine for the last thirty years. We changed our residence so many times but our connection with our milk man continued for ever.

One evening he came to our house and said that he will not be coming for the supply of milk for three days as he had to attend to a marriage in Jallandhar of his close relatives. Three days passed but there was no trace of Anubhav. Two days later I received a phone call from him that three of his close relatives including his young son of 22 years had met a fatal accident in Phagwara and all of them had succumbed to their injuries due to severe crash of the car in which these young boys all students of Engineering college were traveling. The car which was driven by one of them had met with an accident and had hit a stationery truck on the main G T Road. Anubhav was devastated to hear this. He lost his only son and one of his sisters in laws son also died in this accident. No passerby had come to take the victims to the nearby hospital.

All the passerby's who were standing at the site of the accident were only talking in hushed voices as to what had happened and were discussing as to who was at fault. None had the courage and guts to take the bleeding children to the hospital. It was Anubhavs hunch that had the children been taken to some hospital they might have been saved. But it was not to be. On the day of cremation Anubhav had pledged in his mind that if he ever witnessed an accident he will never stop at that site. If no one helped in his grief, why should he help some one else? Anubhav had eaten the bitter pill and had resigned to his fate.

Anubhav had married his daughter Vibha three years after the calamity and was now leading a contented life with his wife Neeti. It was a cold wintry morning and it was raining heavily. He had gone to drop his wife Neeti who was working as a nurse in a Government hospital. On the way back home near a petrol pump he came across a huge motley of young children dressed smartly in their School blazers and a few passerby's who were daily workers who were going on their cycles to look out for work on daily wages. On one side he saw a scooter upside down and two young boys of the age of 15 or 16 bleeding profusely. They looked to be students of plus 1 or plus 2 and it looked as if they had met with an accident.

Anubhav accelerated his car and did not think of stopping near the ghastly site. The whole panorama of his son's death came dazzling in front of his eyes. Not even one person on the earth had helped his son and he thought why he should unnecessarily involve him in this accident. He had to supply milk to his customers. After that he had to be ready at 9 am to reach his office.

After driving his car about 500 meters at a high speed he reversed the car and came to the site of the accident. He could smell his son's breath on seeing the blood oozing out of the two children's head. Immediately the passerby's put the young children in his car. The boys had their Identity Cards dazzling in their neck. Anubhav carried the children to DMC hospital in Ludhiana in the emergency ward. Anubhav got the hospital cards made and also spent the money on medicines and the Doctors fees for putting the stitches. Two hours after the accident he made three frantic phone calls to three different people. Two of the calls were made from the public telephone booths in the hospital. Without telling his name he had informed parents of Kashish Arora and Sunil Singh that their sons had met with an accident but were now out of danger and were ready to be discharged from the hospital.

The third call Anubhav made was to his wife Neeti on her mobile. With tears trickling from his eyes he told his wife in a soaking voice about the accident and how he had BROKEN his pledge not to help any distressed person. By the time parents of Kashish Arora and Sunil Singh came to DMC hospital the GOOD SAMARITAN had fled away without giving his name and mobile number to the hospital authorities. The happiest couple on hearing this sad episode was Anubhavs wife Neeti and Anubhav himself who had broken his vow. Neeti was so proud of her husband that though she lost her only son but her husband had saved lives of two unknown boys. Anubhav's married daughter Vibha was so happy that she could never tie Rakhi to her brother but Kashish Arora and Sunil Singh sisters would tie the sacred thread to their brothers.

Happiness is but an Occasional Episode in the General Drama of Pain

It is very difficult to define happiness. It is very easy to feel it Happiness is something which money cannot buy. A person may be having lakhs of rupees in his FDR account but he may not be happy. Happiness is something which has to come from within. A person may be having good money with him but if he does not enjoy good health and does not have peace of mind than that money is of no use to him. Similarly a student may be studying very hard but if he does not get good marks then he is not happy. A student will feel very happy if he is able to achieve the target which he or his parents have set. If the child is able to get admission in engineering or medical college naturally the student and his parents will feel happy. We must think of those times when our Madams gave us with STARS on our notebook and we would show it to our parents. Getting a star or "very good" from our teacher inflated our pride and we as students were very happy when we showed our note book to our parents and they were more happy than us.

To some watching a cricket match at the dead of night gives them great pleasure. If the match is between India and Pakistan it gives immense pleasure. Who can forget the 6 deadly sixes hit by Yuvraj Singh in a cricket match between India and England? And the bowler to suffer was no mean bowler. Watching Joginder Sharma a non entity from Haryana doing the last over in twenty 20 match against Australia was a treat to watch. This gave more happiness to cricket lovers than having Rupees ten thousand in their pockets.

To some listening to music gives them great happiness. While listening to old songs of Kishore Kumar & Mohd. Rafi gives more happiness to a music lover. When you are in a low or pensive mood try listening to music all by yourself. There are hundred of songs which give you more happiness than even money can buy.

A rich man having 5 cars may get another Innova. He will not feel happy if another car is added in his kitty. But a poor person who owns a bicycle gets very happy when he gets a scooter.

For some persons they are very happy if their article or photograph is published in a newspaper or in some magazine. They daily look for the paper to see if their name is printed in the article which they sent.

Happiness is but an occasional episode in the general drama of pain. Learn to be happy in small things. Learn to give alms to distressed people or the people in pain. Help a stranger in distress or a needy and poor person or donate blood to some one, he will remember you throughout his life. Give Rupees ten thousand as "Shagun" to a rich person he will forget it after a day!!

P.S. Money cannot buy you happiness. Doing a selfless act to brighten someone's day can make you happy.

The Face Book Friends

Sandy was tall, dark and handsome. He had done his schooling from Sherwood College Nanital. He was the pampered child of his parents who were doing flourishing business in Jallandhar. The parents of this boy probably made a mistake of their life time in marrying this handsome young boy at a young age of twenty one. He was married to Dora a girl from a mediocre family from a remote village in Punjab. The only saving grace of the girl was that she was extremely beautiful.

Everything went on smoothly. The couple was blessed with two children a boy and a girl. After the unfortunate death of father of Sandy at a young age of 50, the business of the family started downward trend. There was a time when the family owned a fleet of 6 cars. Now the time had come when Sandy had no one to keep his head to weep.

Dora had joined the circle where the ladies indulged in full gossip and card session. She had started caring two hoots for her husband. The day she started her card session, she was losing or winning Rs 100 only. It gradually increased to Rs 500 and then Rs 1000. There were days when she lost Rupees 10000 per session. The poor husband had to feel the brunt. Dora had no qualms when she stole the money from the valet of her husband. She even threatened to call the police at night if he refused to give her money.

Sandy could not pay back the loan installments of his bank. The poor fellows name came into cibil and he was being denied loan from all banks as he had become a defaulter.

Clever Dora had got the flat transferred to her name. She had also transferred the car in her name. The worst was yet to come. The children by this time were 6 and 8. Sandy was left with no alternative but to file for divorce against his wife Dora. The king once upon a time had become a pauper now. The poor fellow was thrown out of his own house. He had now to live in a one bed room flat having his grub at Highway dhaba's. Gone were the days of Kings Hotel where Christina worked as a manager.

Christina from Goa was a lively lady of thirty five. She was from a rich business family. Both of her brothers were doing roaring business but her two sisters in law were bent upon turning Christina out of her maternal house.

Christina had married a Punjabi boy Aditya of Amritsar. It was a fairy tale wedding. Their foreign tour included visits to Singapore, Malaysia, London, Paris, New York and many more. They were blessed with two girls now aged 5 and 7.

What once upon a time was a fairy tale wedding was turning out to be a journey on thorns. The small fights, the big fights and then the biggest fight in the court room at

Amritsar. Christina had no one to accompany to the court room except her old mother of 67 years. Her brothers and sisters in laws refused to accompany her at court. The girls were too young to understand the agony of their parents.

It's an old saying that no one is as good as whitewashed by his friends and no one is as bad as painted black by his enemies. Christina was painted black not only by her husband Aditya but also by her in laws. She was made to stand as a victim in the court of law.

The divorce was granted as a compromise and out of court settlement. The girls were given to Aditya and poor Christina walked out of her house from Amritsar to Jalandhar all alone. She could have claimed alimony but she did not claim anything, not even her children!!!

Christina came to her mother's place in Jalandhar. Her mother had a palatial house in Jalandhar in a posh locality of Model Town. She cooked her own food. She was afraid to use the Air Conditioner at her mother's place. The mother Raj got her will made and gave equal share to Christina and her two brothers. The brothers got an inkling of this and got the will changed. The poor mother Raj, had bequeathed her share to Christina but the brothers and their wives could not stand this.

Christina one night walked out of the house and took a rented accommodation at Defence colony in Jalandhar. Depressed but well dressed. She had no one to fall for. She had been shunted out from her husband's home, deprived love of her children, forced out of her paternal home and no relatives to support her.

Christina only friend in life was internet and face book. Through face book she came in contact with Sandy a depressed person who had started from a scratch once again. He started the business of interior decorator and was working in his factory till 10 pm. He was almost on the verge of suicide. Sandy had no friend but his philosophy in life was: *Take one step at a time.* Christina was excellent in public relations and she was booking marriage functions, kitty parties, couple kitties etc in her hotel. She was getting handsome pay.

Christina was getting offers from her friends for remarriage. Once bitten twice shy. She was now looking for a husband who was rich and might be ugly. Only money was her consideration. She had been defeated in life once in her fairy tale wedding and did not want to take chance again.

After spending long hours in chatting and poking Sandy on facebook, one day she gave her phone number to Sandy. He would talk to Christina for long hours on net telling her about his problems in life. He talked about his wife, his children and his riches to rag story. Christina also shared her joys and sorrows over the net. No one proposed to each other. Though both had liking for each other. Both were mentally ruined and were looking for resurrection in life.

A chance meeting with Doctor Gupta at Ludhiana clinched the issue. He was a top Psychologist at Ludhiana. Both of them had come to his clinic to get their problem solved. Out of blue the song from DDLJ – "*Tujhe dekha to yeh jaana sanam*" clinched the issue for them.

LO
VE

LOVE & HATE RELATIONSHIP

I was not born in Pakistan. But I have always shared a love and hate relationship with this country. I am no politician but a common man. Since I am born after Partition I had no idea about how the cities like Lahore looked. My father had graduated from Lahore college and my grand father had worked as a Sub Judge in Lahore. I had a burning desire to see Lahore. The first Passport which I made was in the year 1990 which got expired in the year 2000 with no travel entry.

I had decided not to renew the passport again as I had no chance to see a foreign land. When I went to Gurdaspur as Vigilance Officer in my Bank, I became friendly with a Manager whose brother was in SGPC. He told me that he can help me in getting Pakistan visa. That was in the year 2004. He told me just to give my Passport & three photographs. Rest all the formalities will be completed by him. Without telling my better half and my children I gave my Passport to my Banker colleague of Batala. Almost three months after that one day I got a call from Batala that I had got Visa for Pakistan for ten days to visit religious places. In the mean time my son was working in USA. He was sending me papers for my tourist visa.. A bird in hand is better than two in a bush. This famous quote I had learnt from my maternal grandfather. On one hand I had a visa for Pakistan and on other hand I was looking for a visa to America. When I told my wife that I intend to visit Pakistan with a Sikh Jatha she was flabbergasted. Getting first stamp of Pakistan on my Passport meant that I will never get visa for America. That was the perception of people around me. However after much deliberation, I took the plunge and embarked on my journey to Lahore in a Train to Pakistan in April 2004.

What followed was a ten day Journey to various places in Punjab of Pakistan, visiting Lahore, Nankana Sahib, Panja Sahib & Kartarpur . The love and hospitality we Indians received was immense. There looked to be no difference in the streets of Lahore and Delhi. At both the places the streets are crowded & at both places you get street food which is relished by Punjabis on both sides of the border. Since I was on a religious journey I did not taste the non vegetarian food which was available in plenty in food courts of Lahore. But I enjoyed the Indian delicacies like Puri, Chane, Halwa, Lassi etc. The shopping was a treat to do. The shopkeepers kept on pestering us with tea, cold drinks and some even offered us sweets since we were their guest of honor. There was not even an iota of hostility which we so often read in newspapers and see on the electronic media of both the countries. It was real safe to travel all alone even at midnight in Lahore in a three wheeler to taste the Nawabi food and listen to the Indian songs from movies like Pakeeza in full blare.

The Pakistani girls and women loved anything which was Indian especially the

Indian Bindis & Indian suits & saris. I had taken a few packets of Bindis which I gave to the girls and women of Pakistan. They were so thankful to receive these small gifts from unknown visitors from India. When we entered Pakistan border we were cheered by the Pakistan crowd as if we were a VIP. All the Indians were garlanded by people of Pakistan when we entered the Sarai in Nankana Sahib. I did not stay in a luxurious five star hotel and did not get an AC. On the other hand we stayed in a room occupied by six or seven people and that too slept on a floor. But we were completely bowled over by the hospitality of their common people.

After this Pakistan visit I got USA visa for ten years and have visited America three times and have stayed there for almost seven months visiting length and breadth of that country. Americans are very free and very friendly and there is so much to see and explore there. But still out of the nine countries which I have visited till date I find my stay in Pakistan as the most memorable. I would love to visit this country again and again.

But I have not been able to fathom out that why in India versus Pakistan cricket match I always want India to win. Also in Kabaddi and Hockey I want Indians to win against Pakistan irrespective of the strength of our team. But when Pakistan wrestlers and boxers are fighting against Iran or Kazakhstan in Asian Games I always cheer for the Men in Green. It was Hamlets dilemma for me why I was so happy to see Sania Mirza, Pakistani Bahu to win the Gold in Asian games in Mixed doubles in Lawn Tennis !!!!

PS: The two sides of the same coin.

Everyone wants to go Green

One More Reason to Fight

Sometime around late 1990's I was under the wrong impression that my boss never fought with his wife. I was flabbergasted when he told me the reasons. The funniest reason which he told me was that his wife fought with him because he always came early from the office. Then I was under the wrong notion that my subordinates never fought with their better halves. Here again I was proved wrong when each of my subordinates told a long story about the reasons of their quarrels. A common reason given by them was that their wives fought because they always came late from the office. I always thought that businessmen led a very comfortable life and they must be the happiest person in the world. But while talking to a businessman's wife, I was astonished that the young lady said that her husband always goes to the factory at 9 a.m. and return not before 10 p.m. That was another reason for them to fight. What about the poor people? Were they happy without any bickering? I was astonished when their wives grumbled that their husbands never went to work and were always busy in playing cards and drinking. The silliest notion which I had was film personalities like Amitabh and Jaya were an ideal couple. I was shocked, when I read in a popular paper that Rekha in her late fifties still harbored a keen desire for Amitabh. If Rekha is around, can Amitabh and Jaya be an ideal couple?

I have recently taken car loan from the Bank. I had thought that all my ordeals were over now. But infact it was the beginning of my ordeals. Neither me nor my better half knew how to drive a car. So it was a long fifteen days course in a driving school for both of us. We had to shell out around Rs four thousand for car driving training for myself, my better half and my son. As soon as we got the "passing out" certificate from the driving school the real drama began. When I was at the wheels, my wife and son wanted to drive the car. When they were at the wheel, it was my turn to ask for the steering seat. My son wanted to impress with his fast driving. So it was always a game of sitting at the wheel for every one of us. I wanted to go to the office in the car. So did my wife wanted to go to the kitty party or bazaar in the car. My son was not behind, when he wanted to go to his college in car or wanted to go for a haircut around 20 kms from the house in the car. When I wanted to drive slowly, they wanted the car to run at high speed and vice versa when they wanted it slow, I wanted the car to be driven at high speed. There was always a quarrel when every one of us sat in our car.

To avoid this situation now I have decided once for all that one car (which I can hardly afford at present) is not enough for me. As such I have decided to buy two more cars – separate cars for my wife and my son.

Any bank willing to give me a loan ? We will see – playing the waiting game.

MBA AFTER VRS

It was the best of times for some. It was the worst of times for others. The banks were magnanimous enough for announcing the VRS – Voluntary Retirement Scheme for all its employees. Some banks had given the option that they will retire/leave all those people who opt for this "golden opportunity". Other banks were cautions enough and they did not go for mass VRS. They refused to "relieve" bright clerks / officers / AGM / DGM etc and those employees who were 50 years of age. For two long months when the scheme came in newspaper in the form of circular from the banks, there were meetings and counter meetings inside the bank premises, in the Zonal office, in the Head office, infact everywhere.

Self appointed "leaders" who could work out the "pros" and "cons" of VRS gave deafening speeches. Anyone who had opted for this scheme made sure that at least one or two persons of his clan joined him.

The banks received applications under VRS in thousands. Some of the employees who had opted for VRS were under the impression that the management will crush them when so many employees will leave the bank.

But nothing like that happened. A branch, which "boasted" of seven managers, was left with only one manager and the working of that branch had improved in the next month.

There were both the pros and cons of VRS. No doubt the employees had to work harder and in trying circumstances but there was promotion galore in all the banks. Officers became Managers within 7 years and Manager became a Senior Manager in a short span of 5 years.

A colleague of mine had infact filled his VRS application much before the last date for submission of the same. He was "wise" enough. He had given strict instructions to his wife that if anything happened to him before the cutoff date for submitting the application she must submit the application to the higher authorities before performing his "last rites". Horror of Horror that same guy is now the Senior Manager of a prestigious bank in a prestigious place.

Another person who had taken VRS in fact got 20 lakhs plus pension but he didn't know how to "pass" his time. He used to come daily to the branch where he worked and made innumerable calls just to kill his time.

The most disgusting part of VRS employees is when some friend / relative ask him where he/she is working? Why did he go for VRS when his kids are still small.

One of the best answers came from such employee – he has taken VRS from bank but not from home as his wife doesn't allow him to sit at home. She says that he must be out of the house at 9:30 A.M. and should not enter it before 6:00 P.M.

The funniest answer came from another bank employee. When asked what VRS meant to him? Pat came the reply ---it is "VAHLEY REHAN DI SCHEME"

Another inquisitive person when asked what were his plans after VRS. He quipped, I will be doing MBA after VRS i.e. attending "MARRIAGES", "BHOGS" and "AKHAND PATHS". He look forward to attend at least 25 MBA's in coming months.

My Friend Ila

Hello, is it 271115? Ravi asked, "Yes, may I know whom do you want on line" said Ila. If the answer was from the one he wanted, he would talk with her for quite some time. But if the phone was picked by her sister, or her parents he would put the receiver down. This phone business had continued for more than six months. Ravi did not have the courage to tell Ila about his feelings. Ravi was working in a senior level in a private Bank. He had very few friends. But if he made some friends they were of lasting nature. Ravi was basically an introvert. On the other hand his wife Mini was a fun loving lady. She made friends easily.

Mini was teaching in a Convent. She had recently been transferred from Lucknow to

Jammu on her husband's promotion. It was her first year in school but she made friends easily. She came in contact with Saru. Saru was also bereft of friends. She was a soft spoken petite lady with perfect manners. She looked every inch a compere on a T.V.

That day Saru was very happy. Her sister Ila was to get medal on the Republic Day. The medal was to be presented by the Governor. Ila was exactly opposite to her sister. She was a fun loving girl. Nobody could make from her face that she also suffered from some deep problem.

Ravi was greatly impressed by Ila. In fact it was Ravi's wife Mini who had introduced Ila to her husband. That day Mini was talking to her friend Saru and her sister Ila. All of a sudden Ravi's car swept across them and he made a screeching halt. Mini as usual was her naughty self and said "what makes you put your brakes in front of 3 ladies". Ravi just laughed. Saru pleaded with Ravi to come to their house for snacks. There he got introduced to Saru's sister Ila.

Ila was a young lecturer working in a college nearby and teaching Psychology. She cracked jokes at the expense of her sister and her friend. She said that she had seen most of the country in her NCC career.

Ravi got the phone number of Ila through his wife. He would continue to talk with her when no one was around. There were talks on psychology, literature, politics and sports. Whenever Ravi was free, he would dial 271115.

Ravi was once in a jovial mood and asked Ila whether throughout her life she would remain single. To this she just put the receiver down. Ravi felt agitated throughout the day, that why he had hurt the feelings of a young lady. When he came from the Bank that day he suddenly asked Mini "What is wrong with Ila. What makes her allergic to marriage?" Mini did not reply and changed the topic.

Ravi was bent upon finding the truth. That night at 11 pm, he again rang 271115. After a minute it was Ila on the other side with a husky "Hello". "Hi" said Ravi. Ila felt sorry for her behavior previous day and apologized for putting the receiver down that day.

"Ravi I would tell you everything what you want to know about my life. You are one good friend in which I will confide about myself. You are one person who has understood me and nor degraded me. I doubt if you know that I was married about 5 years back said Ila. There was no remorse in her voice. "*Then*?" Ravi said, inquisitive to know about the truth soon.

"My husband was a doctor - a very reputed one whom the patients revered. But his parents and he always degraded me. There was no one in their family whom I could look upon as my own. My husband Anil was always busy either in his work or with the lady doctor and nurses. I felt so neglected during my six months stay in their house that I wanted to run away from life. I had decided either to live honorably or quit. Anil and I moved court for separation with mutual consent.

The divorce was granted after about 2 years. After that my life's attitude changed. I am working as lecturer in a college maintaining my car and living comfortably with my parents and sister.

"Indeed a courageous girl - Bravo Ila" Ravi said and put the receiver down and decided not to call 271115 ever again till he found a suitable partner for his friend Ila.

PS: Marriages are made in Heaven but celebrated on earth.

BUTTER

SWEET TEMPTATIONS

Aridaman had just returned from foreign tour of USA. Aridaman had gone with his wife Pooja to stay with his son and daughter. The three months period passed in no time. The family went to Las Vegas, Seattle, Eugene, New York, and Grand Canyon. Aridaman and Pooja were seen off at San Francisco airport by their son Arvind and daughter in law Anjali. The partings are always tough! Especially when the parents knew that they will not be meeting their children for another year.

Aridaman had just retired from bank after completing 35 years of service. He was a carefree man leaving all the responsibilities to his wife Pooja. His only job in his life was to work and then give the pay packet to his wife on the last Thursday of every month. It was for the wife to pay all grocery bills, the telephone bill, the car petrol bill and other necessary evil bills. The motto of Aridaman was to enjoy life to the fullest especially after the retirement and settling of children. Pooja was still working as a teacher in a prestigious school in Ludhiana. The neighbors in the locality sometimes would say: Aridaman Kamai "*works and slogs*" and Pooja Lootai "*wastes money*".

After landing in Delhi on 22nd January the couple proceeded to their hometown after a memorable three month stay in the United States. It was their third visit to USA. Aridaman and Pooja were greeted on phone by their relatives and friends.

Pooja had to join her school on 25th of January. On 26th of January Aridaman after coming from a morning walk felt a bit uncomfortable. In a casual way they went to Dr. Ohri who checked his BP. BP was almost normal. To be doubly sure Doctor suggested having ECG. But Aridaman was reluctant. Throughout his life he had never been to a doctor for a serious ailment. He never took drinks or smoked cigarettes. He was a regular fitness freak who would go for a regular morning walk. At last the ECG was taken and it showed abnormal signs. Doctor Ohri told Pooja that there was some problem in ECG which needed further investigation in specialized Heart Institute.

On 28th January Aridaman himself drove the car and went to the hospital with his wife. Doctor Mohan advised three tests immediately. The first test was ECG which showed some abnormality. Then it was ECHO test which confirmed that there was serious problem. Doctor Mohan advised admission immediately in the prestigious hospital of Ludhiana.

The phone calls were made to close relatives and friends and colleagues of Pooja. The colleagues of Pooja immediately rushed to the hospital. Brothers and sisters of Aridaman and Pooja rushed to Ludhiana.

Pooja immediately informed her son Arvind and daughter in law Anjali. Arvind was so confused to hear about his Papas illness that he did not know what to do. It was Anjali who took the decision. He got Arvinds air ticket booked to India. It was only a week back that Arvind and Anjali had bid their parents "Bon Voyage". Arvind, a software engineer immediately informed his company about the emergency. The next available flight was taken by Arvind to see his ailing father. Anjali went to the airport to bid " Bon Voyage" to her hubby. Arvind had always seen his father in a jovial mood. Never had he expected that he will see his father in a hospital with grown up beard, in hospital green attire, with glucose. Within 24 hours he was at Ludhiana. He had dashed straight from the Delhi airport to Ludhiana hospital with prayers in his mind. During young age Arvind had fought with his father a number of times over small issues. Mother Pooja was always there to reconcile. On the other hand Anjali was all alone in USA praying for her father in laws good health.

Doctor Mohan fixed up angiography on the next day. The doctor called Arvind who was outside the operation theatre that there was blockage of all arteries. Stunt would not do.

The verdict by the Doctor was given that there would be open Heart Surgery on 4th February.

During the intervening days the money was to be arranged which was to be deposited in the hospital before the operation. The blood bottles had to be arranged. The guests who had come from far off places had to be looked after. Aridaman had never been admitted to the hospital before. He was totally brain washed by the team of head surgeon Doctor, anesthetic and junior doctors. Doctor said that it was a complete safe operation in India with a success rate of about 100 percent.

Pooja's sister Renu visited the hospital three days before the operation. She had promised Aridaman that the operation will go well successfully. But when sorrows come they do not come alone. Renu got severe heart attack in Delhi on 2nd February and she was no more. This news was never told to Aridaman. Doctor Mohan had told all the relatives not to tell this news to the patient. Pooja could not attend the cremation of her sister which was two days after this date. Arvind went to Delhi to attend the cremation and returned on the same day.

3rd February was the birthday of Aridaman. He had never expected to celebrate the birthday among Doctors, Nurses, Ward boys and relatives. This was probably the first time that no cake was cut on Aridaman's birthday, no dinner party with Pooja and children, no receiving of phone calls, no net and no gifts.

The only smell was a typical hospital smell which only a patient and his close relatives could smell. Aridaman gave Victory sign from his bed to his son Arvind and wife Pooja. All the doctors, nurses, ward boys; relatives were greeting the birthday boy.

Doctor Mohan who had worked under Dr. Trehan had vast experience in his medical line. He was daily performing two or three such operations. But an operation is an operation whether a small or a serious one. The patient is under the Doctor's knife for four to five hours with complete anesthesia. Aridaman had been close friend with Dr Mohan's father. Dr Mohan's responsibility to his patient increased when the father told his son about his friendship to the retired banker.

Aridaman was taken to the operation theatre on 4th February a day after his birthday at sharp 9 A.M. Seeing his son, wife and other relatives with his moist eyes, he entered the operation theatre with chanting of Almighty's rhymes. What happened for the next six hours was unknown to Aridaman. Only the relatives knew that the operation was successful and all blockages were removed. Arvind, Pooja and other relatives heaved a sign of relief. He was discharged from the hospital after thirteen days.

After a month with great difficulty, Pooja broke the news to Aridaman of Renu leaving them for heavenly abode. Aridaman could never believe it. She had been his favorite sister in law and she had given him a lot of blessings and courage to him to face the troubled times. But he never thought that he would never meet Renu again. Such is Life – unpredictable and harsh, at times.

After two months another news was in store for Aridaman. Aridaman's son who was back in U.S.A emailed his father that "Papa, while you were being operated, we were having grilled sandwiches in SWEET TEMPTATIONS – a nice joint near the hospital! " giving justification that "*he was hungry*". Aridaman was shocked and emailed back that "*while his father was being cut at the operation theatre, how could he cut the sandwich*, to which he replied back – "*Go to the joint and try it out yourself*". After few days Aridaman along with Pooja made it a point to visit this nice joint and ordered grilled sandwiches. The sandwiches stood by its joint name – Tempting and the incident of having them at the "*time*" became a sweet memory for the family.

PS: The love of family is the greatest love of all.

The Last Ride Together

Bipan Jha had retired from Electricity Board of Assam ten years back. He was leading a comfortable retired life in Paltan Bazar of Guwahati. He was the President of the Senior Citizen Society, which used to meet on every Saturday in a Park near Fancy Bazaar. The members of the society consisted of old and not so old men who were all well placed in life during their career. Some of them were Retired Colonels, another group was of Retired Bankers and some of them were businessmen.

Every Saturday the group of Senior Citizens met over a cup of tea and few snacks sharing their life experiences. Bipan Jha had never been out of the North Eastern States throughout his life. At the age of 68 when he received call from his son Manik that he was sending his ticket along with that of his wife to Montreal his joy knew no bounds. His son Manik was working in Canada for the last eight years in an insurance company. About five years back Manik had got married to a girl from Punjab. It was love at first sight. Manik had met Preeti in Canada. Both of them convinced their parents and the marriage was solemnized in Guwahati. Preeti was a fashion designer and was doing pretty well. She had stayed in Canada all her life. Her parents had migrated to Canada about forty years back and were in transport business.

Manik had got Canadian Citizenship on account of his marriage to Preeti. Manik had filed the papers for his father Bipan Jha and his mother. The D date for departure was set. All the members of Senior Citizen Club gave a hearty farewell to their President Jha. Jha had got permanent residency for Canada. He had initially decided to visit Montreal for six months with his wife.

Bipan Jha and his wife were traveling to Canada and in fact by air to a foreign land for the first time. They had got many instructions from their son and daughter in law. Manik and Preeti were there at the airport to receive their parents. Bipan Jha and his wife Savitri were so happy to be the guest of honors of their son and daughter in law.

All weekends were booked for site seeing in and around Montreal. The family visited so many Malls, a few temples and even one or two Gurdwara's. Manik and Preeti had taken a few days off from their hectic schedules to show Niagara Falls to their parents. It was heavenly to visit one of the seven wonders of the world. The atmosphere of Niagara Falls can only be felt.

Manik had made it a point to touch his parent's feet whenever he went out for work early in the morning. Almost three months had passed. Manik's parents were so delighted to see the progress made by his son and daughter in law. Bipan Jha had been in contact with his friends and relatives in India telling them about the places visited and the difference in culture of the two countries.

It was like another day in August. Manik took leave of his parents and bowed in reverence to his parents. He had left the home early at 7 am. Almost one hour after Manik left his home; his wife Preeti received a call from a hospital in Montreal that Manik had suffered a heart attack. No one could imagine that Manik could suffer heart attack at the young age of thirty six. Manik had not been a chain smoker nor a heavy drunkard, except for a few drinks in the office party.

Preeti with her eyes swelling with tears told her in laws about the condition of Manik. All of them immediately rushed to the hospital. The doctors told the family about the condition of young Manik. The family prayed for ten days till Manik was in the hospital. He was kept in a ventilator for the entire ten days.

In spite of the best efforts of the doctors Manik could not be saved. The world of Bipan Jha, Savitri and Preeti was shattered. They, who had decided to stay in Canada for six months were devastated by the sudden development. They could neither stay in Montreal in the house of his son nor could they leave their beloved daughter in law Preeti.

They were in Hamlets dilemma whether to stay back in Montreal or go back to Guwahati. They could not afford to see Preeti in so much grief. Nor could they stay in this beautiful house always looking at the empty rooms and walls. They had no one to fall who could understand their native language. Finally a bold decision was taken by the Jhas.

Bipan Jha and Savitri embarked on plane back to Guwahati after a few days. They could not bear to see Preeti in grief. On the return journey from Montreal to Guwahati they continued to remember THE LAST RIDE TOGETHER which they had taken with Manik two days before. Preeti continues to wait for her in laws when they will come back to Montreal!!!

PS: Life is uncertain, do not take anyone for granted – express your love and care for your loved ones often, you never know when will be their last...

It's easy to give up life
Life's lesson stay strong
Its easy to get lost
Life's lesson find your way
It's easy to loose hope
Life's lesson have faith
It's easy to get bogged down
Life's lesson have patience
It's easy to hate life
Life's lesson spread love
It's easy to fight
Life's lesson fall in love
It's easy to fall
Life's lesson keep moving
It's easy to feel depressed
Life's lesson believe in yourself
Life is not a bed of roses, we know it for long
Every moment is a challenge, lets move along
Gear up buddy, for life is short
Make your every move as if your last....

Thanks to Chhavi Bakshi for penning these beautiful lines.

CPSIA information can be obtained
at www.ICGtesting.com
Printed in the USA
LVHW012029270921
698838LV00017B/2748